EMMELINA AND THE MONSTER

Will clever Emmelina be able to overcome the powerful monster?

June Crebbin was a primary school teacher before taking early retirement to concentrate on her writing. She is the author of a number of books for children, including *The Curse of the Skull*, *Tarquin the Wonder Horse* and the picture books *Fly by Night*, *The Train Ride*, *Danny's Duck*, *Into the Castle* and *Cows in the Kitchen*, as well as several volumes of verse and three titles for beginner readers in Walker Books' Read Me series. A frequent visitor to primary schools, where she gives readings, talks and workshops, June Crebbin lives in Leicestershire with her husband and her rabbit.

Books by the same author

Carrie Climbs a Mountain
Tarquin the Wonder Horse

For older readers

The Curse of the Skull

JUNE CREBBIN

Emmelina and the Monster

Illustrations by Tony Ross

WALKER BOOKS
AND SUBSIDIARIES
LONDON • BOSTON • SYDNEY

For John

First published 1998 by
Walker Books Ltd, 87 Vauxhall Walk
London SE11 5HJ

This edition published 2001

2 4 6 8 10 9 7 5 3 1

Text © 1998 June Crebbin
Illustrations © 1998 Tony Ross

This book has been typeset in Garamond

Printed and bound in Great Britain by The Guernsey Press Co. Ltd

British Library Cataloguing in Publication Data:
a catalogue record for this book is
available from the British Library

ISBN 0-7445-8904-5

Contents

CHAPTER 1

Once, in a hot and distant land, just outside a village, lived a monster.

It had a long, scaly tail like a serpent. It had the head and body of a cockerel, and it ran so fast, it could catch you in an instant.

But that was not its deadliest
power. Oh, no.

Its deadliest power lay in its eyes.

The rule was never, never look
into them.

Now, one day, three sisters,
knowing nothing of this monster,
were travelling towards the village.
Their names were Gina, Dina and
Emmelina, and their parents had
sent them out into the world to seek
their fortune.

Gina was a big thumping girl.
She liked to eat huge quantities of
spaghetti and rich tomato sauce –
and thump people.

Dina was tall and vain. She liked
to wear beautiful dresses and look
at herself in the mirror.

Emmelina was small. She did not
eat much (Gina saw to that), or
wear fine clothes (Dina saw to that),
but she thought a great deal.

As they drew closer to the village,
the sisters came to a cornfield.
A man was cutting the corn. At
least, it looked as if he was cutting.
Certainly he held the scythe with
its shining blade high in the air. But
the blade never fell.

"Lazy fellow!" cried Gina. She tramped across the field and thumped him.

She screamed as her fist struck not skin – but stone.

Then she noticed that all over the field were people who looked as if they were cutting, binding, gathering the corn.

But no one actually moved.

They weren't people, but statues.

"Let's go," said Gina. "I'm ready for my supper."

"But..." began Emmelina. But Gina was already striding up the hill.

On the hillside, they came to a lemon grove. A woman was picking lemons. At least, it looked as if she was picking. Certainly her hand was stretched towards a lemon. But the basket at her feet was empty.

"Oh, goody!" cried Dina. "Lemons! They're so good for my skin. I shall make myself a face-pack straight after supper."

She reached rudely above the woman's head, and touched her arm.

She screamed as her hand met not skin – but stone.

Then she noticed that all over the lemon grove were people who looked as if they were climbing ladders, picking lemons, filling baskets.

But no one actually moved.

They weren't people, but statues.

Gina and Dina were already
hurrying on towards the village.
For the moment, Emmelina could
do nothing but hurry after them.

Close by, the monster stirred
in its nest.

CHAPTER 2

When the sisters entered the village, no one was about. They walked right through it without seeing a soul.

But on the other side of the village, they saw a castle, and in front of its great doors, a beautiful woman was speaking to a crowd of people.

"Who is brave enough to rid us of this monster?" she said.

"What monster?" Emmelina asked a boy standing nearby.

Gina and Dina started to head back the way they had come.

"It lives just the other side of the village," said the boy. "You must never, never look into its eyes, or it will turn you to stone."

Gina and Dina stopped.

Then Gina laughed. "We didn't
see any monster on our way here!"
she said.

"Just be glad it didn't see you first,"
said a woman. "I've lost a husband."

"We saw workers in the fields and in the lemon grove turned to stone,"  said Emmelina. "Is that the monster's doing?"

"Yes," said a man. "We cannot harvest our corn or our fruit."

"And if we cannot harvest," said the woman, "we shall starve."

The beautiful woman, who was the Queen, spoke again. "I will give my castle to anyone who rids us of this monster!"

26

There's bound to be plenty of food in a castle, thought Gina.

There are bound to be plenty of fine clothes in a castle, thought Dina.

"I'll do it!" they both shouted.

"No, you won't," hissed Gina, and thumped Dina so hard, she knocked her out.

"*I'll* do it," said Gina, pushing her way to the front. "But first I must have food and a good night's rest."

The Queen, overjoyed, welcomed Gina and her sisters into the castle.

CHAPTER 3

Inside the castle, the Queen gave
orders for Dina to be taken to the
Blue Bedchamber to recover.

Gina and Emmelina were taken to
the Great Hall for a splendid supper.
Huge plates of pineapple and
pepper pizzas, steaming dishes of
ravioli and spaghetti, olives, grapes
and garlic bread filled the table.

Gina ate heartily, but Emmelina could eat nothing. Though the Queen entreated her to have at least a thin slice of pizza, or a small dish of spaghetti, Emmelina pleaded tiredness and asked to be excused.

A servant showed her to the Red
Bedchamber. Crimson velvet
curtains hung at the windows. On
the floor was a scarlet carpet,
patterned with cherries and plums
and strawberries, and on the table
by the bed was a gold lamp studded
with rubies.

Emmelina climbed wearily into the high bed. It was all so beautiful. But what a mess they were in! Poor Dina, knocked out – and Gina...? How Gina thought she was going to get rid of this monster, Emmelina had no idea. Still, it was very brave of her to offer.

In the Great Hall, Gina reached
for another bunch of grapes – and
laughed to herself. She had no
intention of getting rid of the
monster. She would eat her fill and
leave under cover of darkness.

Now for
my bed.

"Sleep well," said the Queen.
Not likely, thought Gina as a
servant showed her into the Green
Bedchamber.

She walked briskly up and down
the room to keep awake. But the
huge meal she had eaten made her
sleepy. And the great four-poster
bed looked so comfortable.

She sank onto the soft covers –
and fell at once into a deep sleep.

CHAPTER 4

The next morning, when Gina woke, she was horrified to find herself still in the castle. Quietly, she opened the door of her bedchamber.

Outside stood a guard. He drew his sword.

"Let me pass!" cried Gina. But the guard took her to the Queen.

"Now," said the Queen. "Is there anything you need before you go?"

"Yes," said Gina. "I need a suit of armour. Send for the blacksmith!"

She thought that while it was being made, she could escape.

"No need," said the Queen. "I'm sure we have one just your size."

A suit of armour was brought. It was exactly right.

Well, thought Gina, nothing can reach me inside this. I might as well slay the monster and claim the castle. It shouldn't take long.

Gina brought down the visor of her helmet over her face.

She clanked out of the castle.

In the lemon grove Gina found nothing. So she clonked along the road to the cornfield.

Close by, the monster watched and waited.

Up and down clunked Gina, round and round.

She wanted to lift up her visor to see better. But she wasn't that stupid.

Presently, at the side of the field, she noticed a vineyard. Bunches of juicy, black grapes hung from every branch. Her mouth watered.

It would only take a minute.

She lifted up her visor, reached for
the grapes and – up sprang the
monster, lightning zinging from
its glittering eyes into
Gina's own.

At once, her arm stiffened, her eyes glazed over. Her body turned to stone.

Meanwhile, back at the castle, Emmelina was helping to clear away the breakfast things – and Dina, who had recovered, was looking at herself in a mirror …

CHAPTER 5

How beautiful I am, thought Dina as she tried on one dress after another from the Queen's wardrobe. First, a crimson ball gown stitched with pearls, then a royal blue, shimmering with sequins, then a purple velvet edged with fur.

"Look," she said, when Emmelina came to tell her the sad news that Gina had not returned. "I don't know which suits me best, I look so beautiful in all of them."

Emmelina stared.

"The monster must have turned our sister into stone!" she whispered.

"Well, what did you expect?" said Dina. "They should have sent me." She smirked into the mirror.

The Queen came into the bedchamber. "You're wearing my best ballgown!" she cried.

"Only because I'm going to charm the monster," said Dina quickly.

After all, she thought, he's bound to be a Prince really, turned into a monster by a wicked spell. One kiss from me should do it. Then I'll have this castle – and a Prince to marry.

"Is there anything you need before you go?" asked the Queen.

"Oh, no," said Dina. "All I need is my beauty."

"Remember, never, never—" began the Queen.

"I know," interrupted Dina. She swept out of the castle and down to the lemon grove.

In and out of the trees Dina strutted.

"Here, Princey-Wincey!" she called.

She didn't have long to wait.

Ugh! she thought when she caught sight of the monster, he's so ugly. Still, it will be worth it.

She closed her eyes.

"Here I am!" she cried. "One kiss from me will set you free!"

She leaned towards him, pouting her lips. She waited. Nothing happened.

So she opened her eyes and – up
sprang the monster, lightning zinging
from its glittering eyes into Dina's
own. At once, her lips set, her eyes
froze. Her body turned to stone.

Back at the castle, Emmelina was
carefully hanging up the clothes
Dina had dropped on the floor...

CHAPTER 6

That night, after Dina had not returned, Emmelina did not sleep. She thought really hard.

"You must never, never look into the monster's eyes," everyone kept saying.

She got out of bed and thought some more. It was so unfair. One glance from the monster... She stopped.

That's it. One glance. That's all it would take.

While it was yet dark, she woke the Queen and explained her plan. "The only thing is," said Emmelina, "I need to borrow something."

"No problem," said the Queen, jumping out of bed.

By daylight, Emmelina was hiding behind a tree at the edge of the cornfield with everything she needed.

She watched for the first sign of the monster. But she was very tired. She told herself stories to keep awake.

Towards midday, when she had just got Cinderella to the ball, the air became very still. She strained her eyes. Something was moving through the corn towards her.

She listened.

Swish, swish. The monster was getting closer.

She drew in her breath and stepped out from behind the tree.

Up sprang the monster, lightning zinging from its glittering eyes into – A MIRROR!

The monster was face to face with itself!

The lightning zinging from its eyes struck the mirror and bounced straight back.

At once, its tail hardened, its eyes dimmed. Its body turned to stone.

Emmelina let out her breath. She looked around. All over the cornfield workers were cutting, binding, gathering the corn as if they had never stopped.

"Hey!" called a voice. A figure in armour was moving towards her, but she didn't wait for it to catch up.

As she hurried back to the castle, men and women were climbing ladders, picking lemons, filling baskets in the lemon grove.

"Hi!" called another familiar voice, but she didn't even look round.

The Queen was overjoyed to see Emmelina. Soon the news of the stone monster spread.

A great feast was prepared to which everyone – including Gina and Dina – was invited.

And although Emmelina politely
refused to accept her reward, she
did agree to live in the castle and be
the Queen's adviser.

Gina was given a job in the kitchen
and Dina in the laundry rooms.

Emmelina lived long and happily.
And sometimes, on summer
evenings, she would tell the village
children the story of the monster
and take them down to
the cornfield to show them how,
in the end, the monster had
turned itself to stone.

More  for you to enjoy!

All at £3.99